What Do You Love?

By
Jonathan London

Illustrated by Karen Lee Schmidt

SCHOLASTIC INC.

New York Toronto London Auckland Sydney
Mexico City New Delhi Hong Kong Buenos Aires

ISBN 0-439-38008-1

12 11 10 9 8 7 6 5 4 3 2   2 3 4 5 6 7/0

Printed in the U.S.A.   24

First Scholastic printing, September 2002

The illustrations in this book were done in Windsor Newton watercolors on Arches cold-pressed watercolor paper.

The display and text type were set in Lemonade Regular.

Designed by Judythe Sieck and Carolyn Stafford

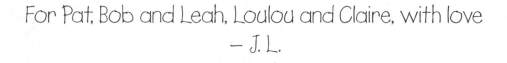

For Pat, Bob and Leah, Loulou and Claire, with love
— J. L.

For Opal and Ivan, mother and son
— K. L. S.

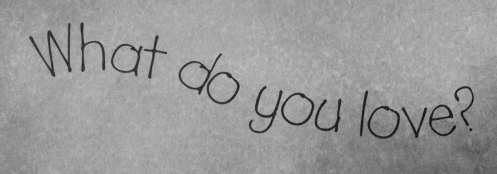

What do you love?

Park slides
and piggyback rides,

mud pies
and Mommy's eyes,

hiding places

and wild chases.

What do you love?

Jumping puddles

and Mommy's cuddles,

big trees and
rustling leaves,

read-alouds

and sunset clouds.

What do you love?

Silly tunes

and full moons,

ice-cream bars
and shooting stars,

long walks
and quiet talks.

What do you love?

Good nights
    and hug-tights,

Mommy's kisses
and bedtime wishes,

moonbeams
and sweet dreams.

What do you love?